MOONCAKE

FRANK ASCH

ALADDIN PAPERBACKS

Revised cover edition, 1999

Aladdin Paperbacks
An imprint of Simon & Schuster
Children's Publishing Division
1230 Avenue of the Americas
New York, NY 10020
Copyright © 1983 by Frank Asch
16 18 20 19 17 15

Manufactured in the United States of America

The Library of Congress has cataloged a previous edition as follows:
Asch, Frank. Mooncake.
Summary: Bear builds a rocket to take him to the moon so he can taste it.
[1. Bears—Fiction. 2. Moon—Fiction.] I. Title.
[PZ7. A778Mpd 1988] [E] 88-6571
ISBN 978-0-689-83517-9
0911 LAK

To Devin
and the Cascos

One summer night Bear and his friend
Little Bird sat down to watch the moon.

After a while Little Bird said:
"I think I feel hungry."
"Me too," replied Bear. "And you know
what I wish? I wish I could just jump up
and take a bite out of the moon. Mmmmmmm,
how delicious that would be!"
"How do you know?" chirped Little Bird.
"Maybe the moon doesn't taste good
at all. Maybe it tastes terrible!"

Bear thought for a moment.
Then he went inside and got his bow
and arrow. With a piece of string,
he attached a spoon to the arrow.

Then he went outside again

and shot the spoon at the moon.

"I knew that wouldn't work,"
said Little Bird.
"The moon is just too far away.
What you need is a rocket ship."
"Then I shall build one!" said Bear.

The very next day Bear went to the junkyard
and bought everything he thought he would need
to build a rocket ship.

All summer long Bear and Little Bird
worked and worked, but when fall came
the rocket ship was still not finished.
"I would like to go with you,"
said Little Bird, "but winter is coming,
and I must fly south with the flock."
So Bear and Little Bird said goodbye.

When it began to get cold and the leaves
fell off the trees, Bear got sleepy.
But instead of climbing into bed and

sleeping through the winter, he kept
right on working. He worked and worked
until the rocket ship was finished.

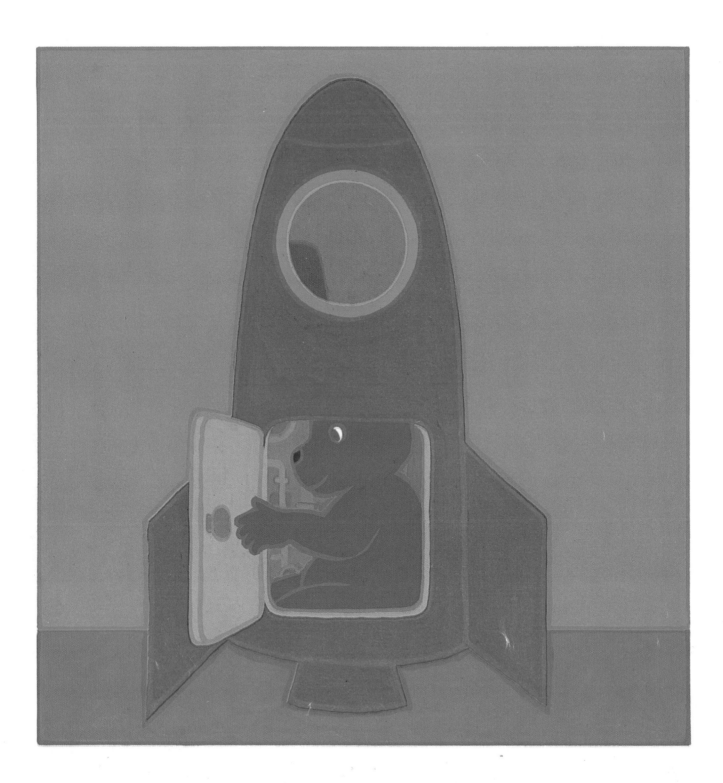

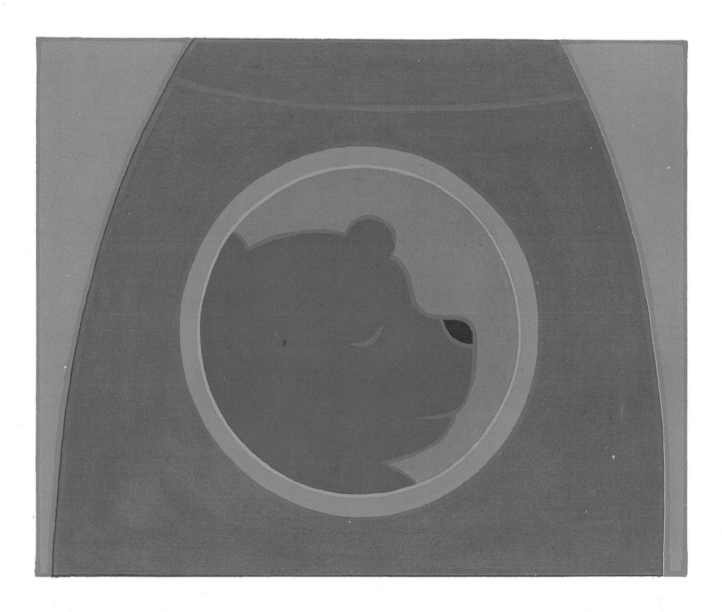

Then he climbed inside and began the countdown:
"10 9 8 7 6 5 4 3 2 zzzzzzz..."
But before he reached 1 he fell asleep.

He slept and slept and slept,

until one night the wind knocked over
his rocket ship.

Bear had never been awake in
the winter before. When he opened
his eyes and saw all the snow,
he thought he was on the moon.
He climbed out of his rocket ship,
scooped up some snow, and made
a little mooncake.
Then he tasted it.
It tasted like something he had
tasted before, but he wasn't quite
sure what it was.

While he thought about that, he decided to go for a walk. He didn't want to go too far, because he was afraid that he would get lost. So he just walked in a big circle. After a while he came upon his own paw prints in the snow.

"These paw prints are too big to belong
to a moon mouse, or even a moon raccoon,"
thought Bear. "Maybe they were made by a
moon bear, or perhaps," he shuddered,
"a terrible moon monster!"
Bear felt scared.
He ran back to his rocket ship
and prepared for takeoff.

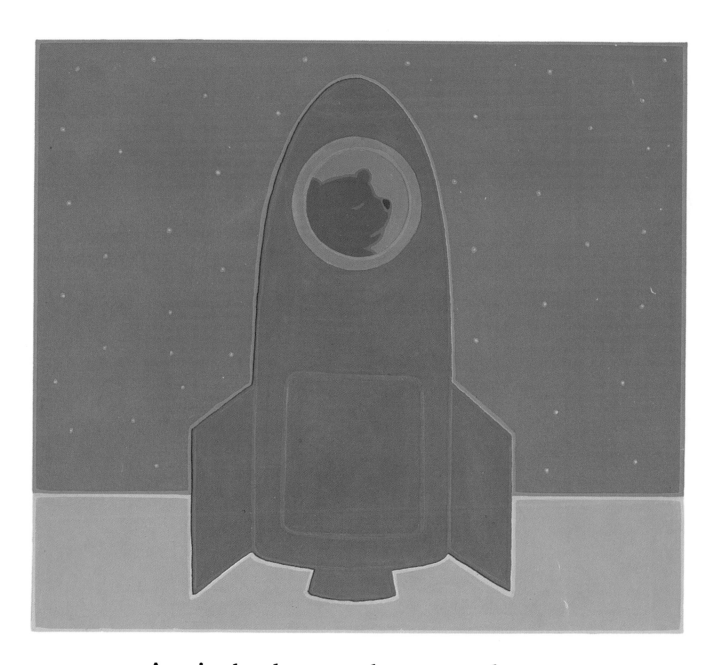

Again he began the countdown:
"10 9 8 7 6 5 4 zzzz...,"
and again he fell asleep.

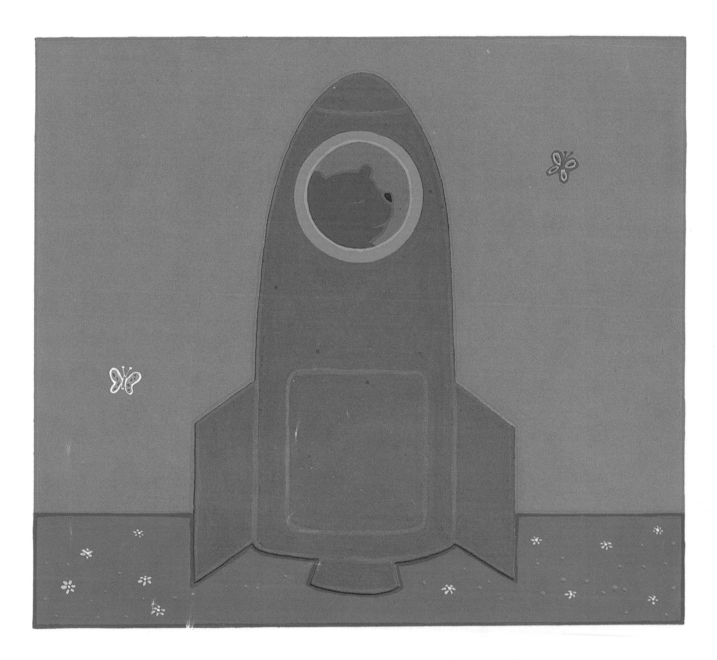

This time he slept until spring.

One day his friend Little Bird returned
and woke him up.
"How was everything down south?" asked Bear.
"Just fine," said Little Bird.
"Did you go to the moon?" asked Little Bird.
"I sure did!" said Bear.

"And how did the moon taste?" asked Little Bird.
"Was it terrible?"
"No," replied Bear, "it was delicious."